Meet Geoffrey, the young giraffe.

He's very, very **tall**,

with a very, very **long** neck . . .

OH DEAR, GEOFFREY!

GEMMA O'NEILL

templar books
an imprint of Candlewick Press

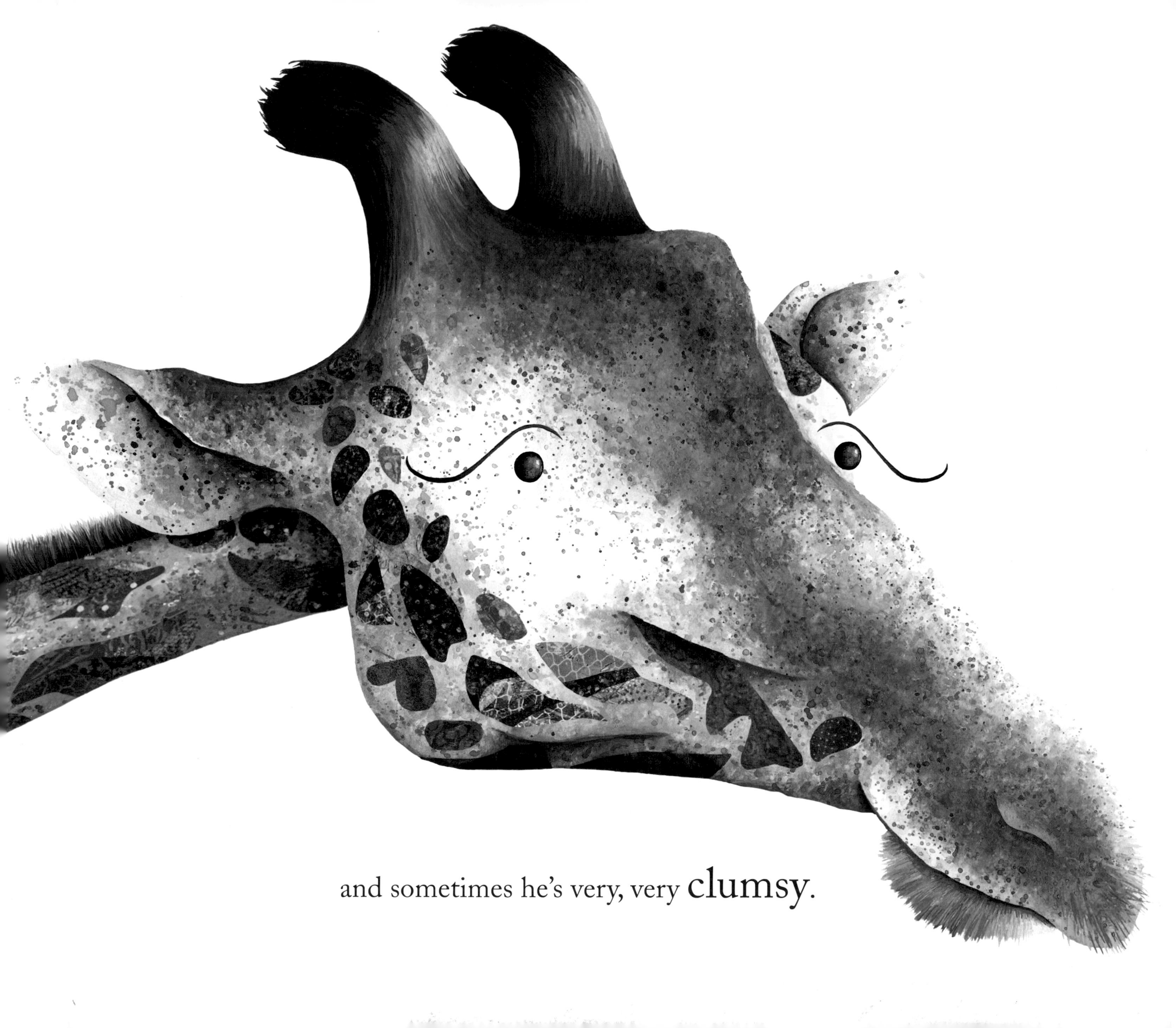

and sometimes he's very, very clumsy.

Meet some more
of Geoffrey.

His legs are wibbly-wobbly . . .

and his knees are bendy-buckly . . .
so he often tangles, trips,
skips, and
flips. . . .

Oh dear, Geoffrey!

Geoffrey bends down as low as he can go
to say hello to the meerkats.

But he slips and slides—and they all disappear in a flash!

Geoffrey won't give up.
He tries to say hello
to the elephants.

But he stumbles,

bumbles,

and bumps!

Soon trunks are tangled and tails are tugged. . . .

Oh dear, Geoffrey!

Down at the watering hole, Geoffrey tries to make friends,
but it's very muddy.

He splishes and sploshes . . .

and then . . .

SPLASH!
Oh dear, Geoffrey!

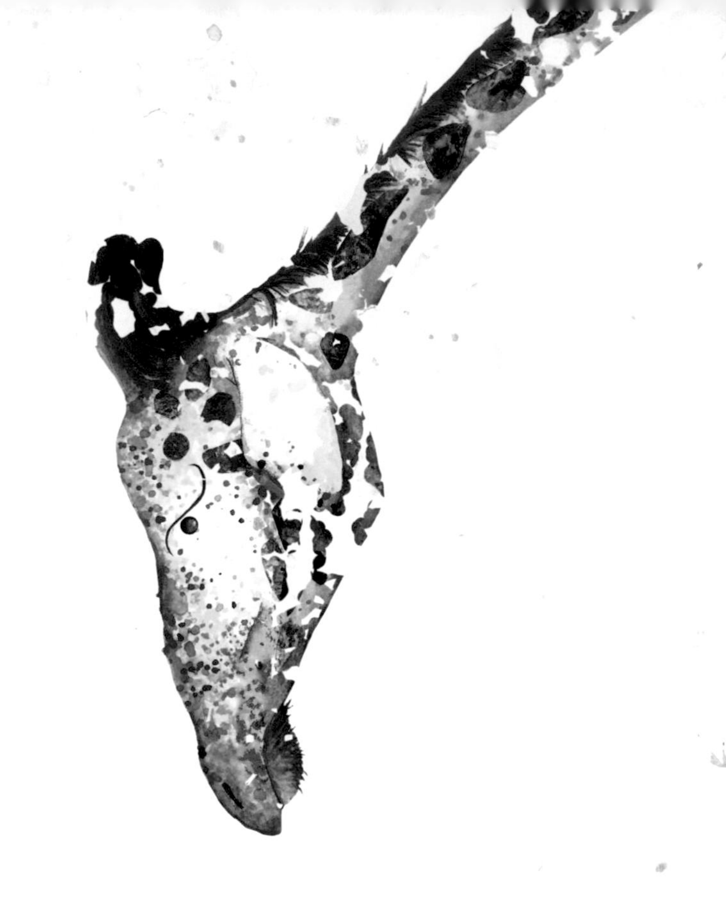

Geoffrey is cold and wet and muddy.

He's fed up with being so tall and clumsy.

So he sets off toward his favorite tree—
the tallest one of all, full of tasty
leaves to cheer him up.

On the way, Geoffrey hears a little voice,
and then he feels something tickly.
He looks down and sees lots of cheeky
monkeys climbing up his legs!

"You're so tall—please will you help us little ones
up to the top of the tree?" they chatter.

Geoffrey lets them all climb up his long neck.

"Thank you, Geoffrey!" say the monkeys.
"Let's be friends!
We would love to have a friend
as tall as you."

“So would we!”

Geoffrey looks around and notices some little birds . . .
right under his nose!

“Nobody else can reach up here where we live.
We’d love to be your friends,”
tweet the birds.

Soon Geoffrey has **more** friends than he can count!

"It's easy to make
friends up here!"
says Geoffrey with a smile.
"And I can stretch as high as I like!"

"You're just like us," twitter the birds.
"You can reach as high as the sky . . .

and see as far as the stars!”

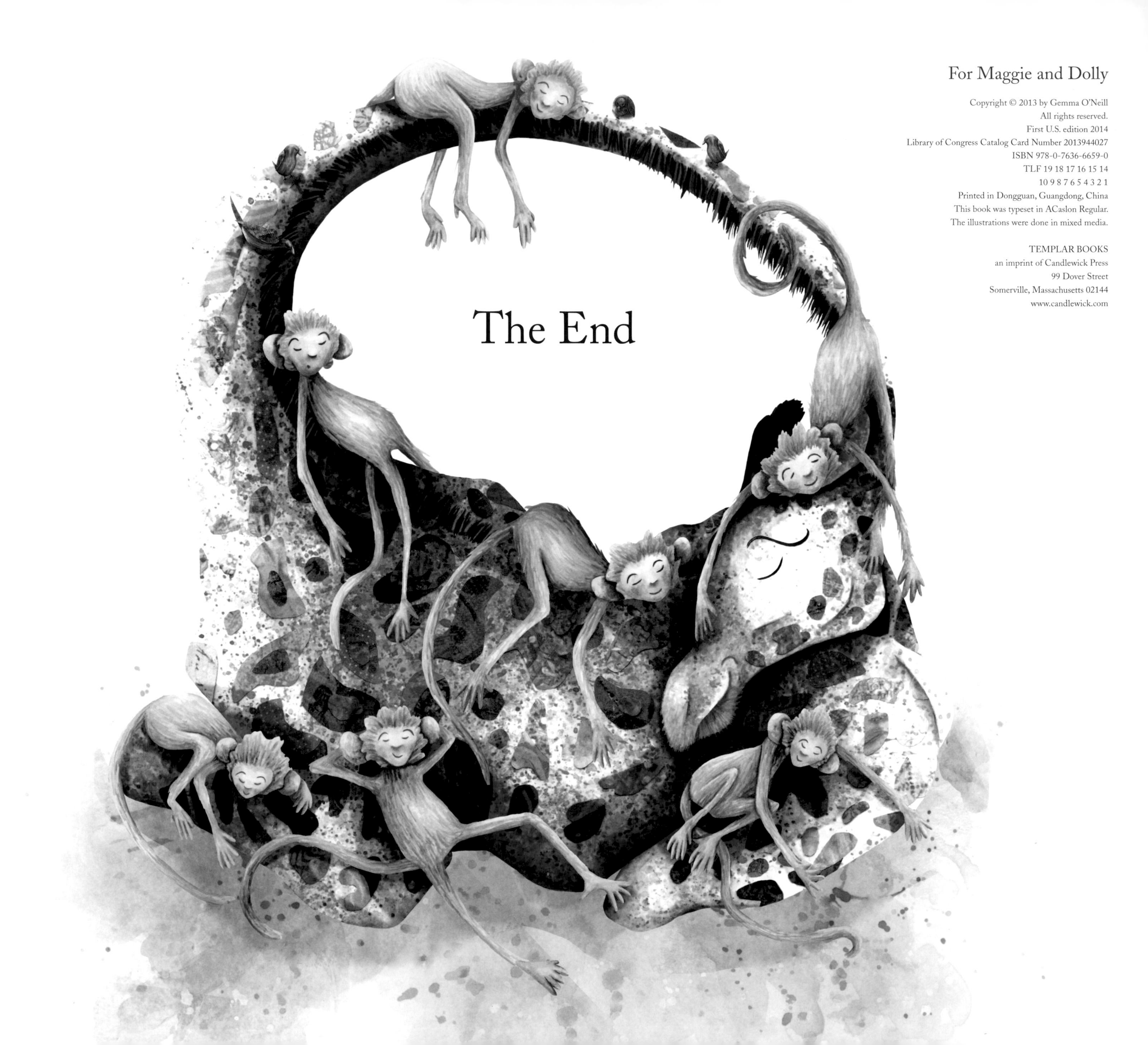

The End

For Maggie and Dolly

First U.S. edition 2014
Library of Congress Catalog Card Number 2013944027
ISBN 978-0-7636-6659-0
TLF 19 18 17 16 15 14
10 9 8 7 6 5 4 3 2 1
Printed in Dongguan, Guangdong, China
This book was typeset in ACaslon Regular.
The illustrations were done in mixed media.

TEMPLAR BOOKS
an imprint of Candlewick Press
99 Dover Street
Somerville, Massachusetts 02144
www.candlewick.com

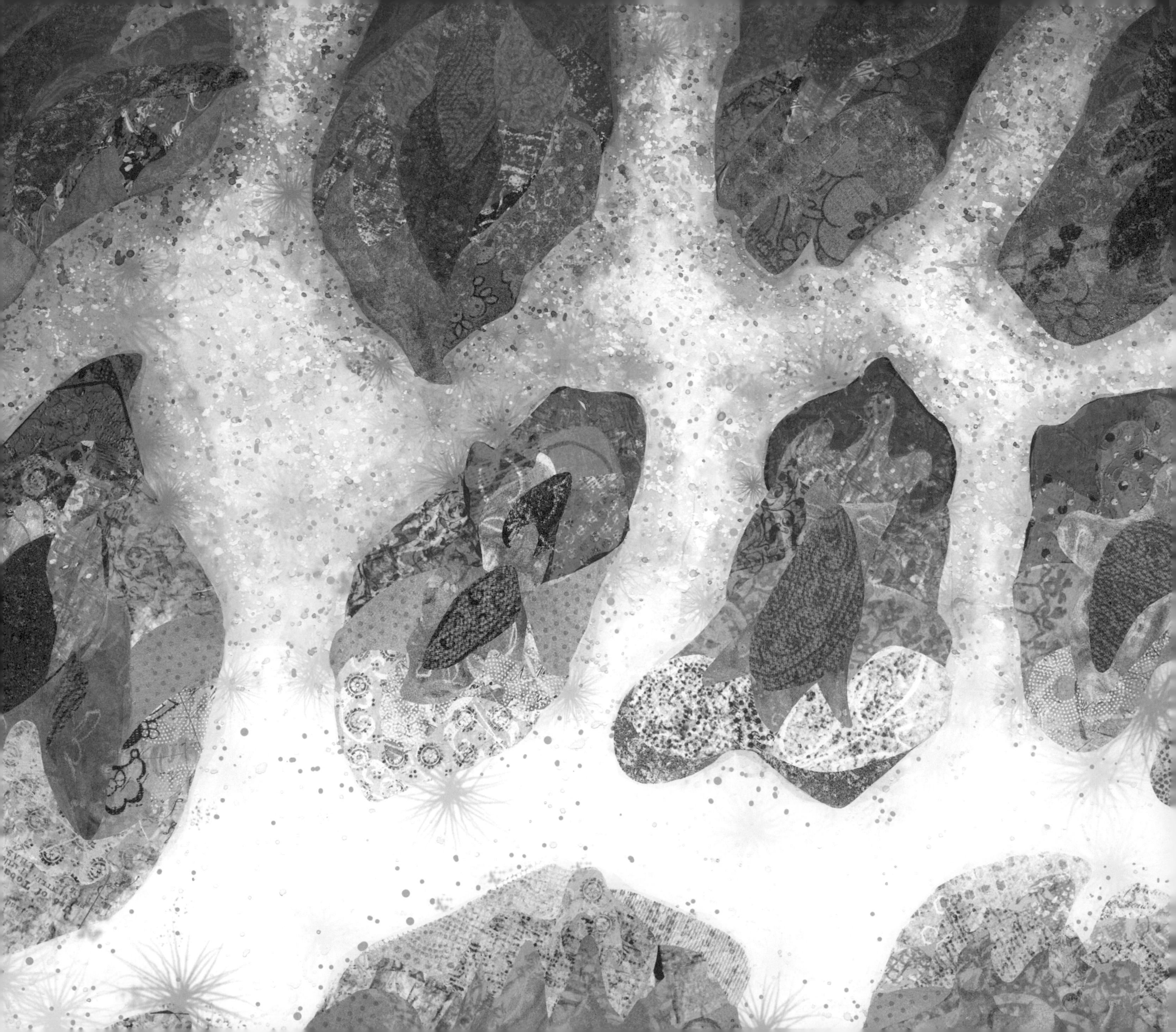